Undone

Hooked book one

Charity Parkerson

Without limiting the rights under copyright(s) reserved above and below, no part of this publication may be reproduced, stored in or introduced into a retrieval system, or transmitted, in any form, or by any means (electronic, mechanical, photocopying, recording, or otherwise) without the prior permission of the copyright owner.

Please Note

The scanning, uploading, and distributing of this book via the internet or via any other means without the permission of the copyright owner is illegal and punishable by law. Criminal copyright infringement, including infringement without monetary gain, is investigated by the FBI and is punishable by up to 5 years in federal prison and a fine of $250,000. Please purchase only authorized electronic editions, and do not participate in or encourage electronic piracy of copyrighted materials. Brief passages may be quoted for review purposes if credit is given to the copyright holder. Your support of the author's rights is appreciated. Any resemblances to person(s) living or dead, is completely coincidental. All items contained within this novel are products of the author's imagination.

--Warning: This book is intended for readers over the age of 18.

Copyright © 2016 Charity Parkerson

Editor: Hercules Editing and Consultants

Photographer: TheArtofPhoto

All rights reserved.

About the Author

Charity Parkerson is an award winning and multi-published author with Ellora's Cave Publishing, Indie Publishing House LLC, and Punk & Sissy Publications. Born with no filter from her brain to her mouth, she decided to take this odd quirk and insert it in her characters.

*2015 Readers' Favorite Award Winner
*Winner of 2, 2014 Readers' Favorite Awards
*2015 Passionate Plume Award Finalist
*2013 Readers' Favorite Award Winner
*2013 Reviewers' Choice Award Winner
*2012 ARRA Finalist for Favorite Paranormal Romance
*Five-time winner of The Mistress of the Darkpath

Connect with her online:

--Website: charityparkerson.com
--Facebook: facebook.com/authorCharityParkerson
facebook.com/TheMenofSin
--Twitter: twitter.com/CharityParkerso

Introduction

Chance didn't expect to start his day in the back of a police cruiser. Lucky for him, the man behind the wheel is Chance's best friend and onetime lover, Jaxon.

Jaxon wants Chance. He has since the first moment he set eyes on the sexy librarian. Unfortunately, Chance always has bullshit going on, standing in their way. Most men would consider Chance more trouble than he's worth. Not Jaxon. He can't get enough of Chance's constant drama. When Chance's life spirals out of control—the way Chance's life always seems to do—Jaxon rushes to the rescue, only to end up screwing things up… again.

These two independent souls might drive each other mad, but there's no denying their love or the fiery hot passion brewing between them. If only Chance could stop lying to Jaxon, maybe they'd stand a chance.

Undone is a short introduction to Charity Parkerson's new M/M series, Hooked.

Chapter 1

He'd always had a weakness for hard bodies. Although a common downfall among anyone possessing sexual organs, Chance had taken his obsession to a whole new level. Two weeks after his eighteenth birthday, he'd walked away from drug-dealing parents who took turns serving time, and straight into the arms of a professional body builder who'd caught his eye. The man had been in Chance's hometown of Chetwood, Alabama working at an author's book signing where he'd been the cover model.

Chance loved books. Adam was on

the cover of several. Insta-book-boyfriend-love had been born. At the time, Chance hadn't seen a problem with running off with the twenty-six-year-old hottie. Of course, there'd been a thousand things he hadn't seen a problem with when it came to Adam Lowe. Loving Adam had made Chance incredibly stupid.

When Chance was twenty-four, while traveling with Adam for a competition, Adam hooked up with another competitor, leaving Chance alone in a strange town where he hadn't known a soul. He'd survived. Chance always survived — somehow.

Now, here he was at twenty-seven,

and Chance would like to believe he'd learned his lesson. The hot ones were always trouble. Of course, he'd also like to think Adam had been his biggest misstep, but no. That honor went to Jaxon West. In this case, it wasn't the other man's fault. Chance was the one who was the idiot in this equation. Jaxon was the only good man Chance had ever fallen for, and Chance was — no doubt — the biggest mess Jaxon had ever encountered. There had been one steamy night between them... Chance turned his mind away from the memory of Jaxon's hands skimming over his skin. Since Chance was currently sitting in the back of a Rutherford County police cruiser, sweating in places God could not have intended, he didn't need to go there. Jaxon was behind the wheel, making it that much harder. Pun intended. Yep. It was like that. He'd forced Jaxon to extremes.

"I'm not mad at you," Jaxon said for the third time, making Chance absolutely sure he was indeed angry with him. If Jaxon wanted to convince himself otherwise, then Chance was on board with the plan. Whipping the car to the side of the road, Jaxon cut off several other vehicles. Horns blared as he threw the car in park. "Fuck that," he added, spinning in his seat and glaring at Chance through the partition. "I'm fucking furious. Why in the hell didn't you call me the moment that big-ass motherfucker started banging on your door?"

Chance shrugged, incapable of looking Jaxon in the eye. "I don't know." It was a blatant lie, of course. There were a thousand reasons why Chance hadn't called Jaxon for help. They all began with how blue Jaxon's eyes were and ended with how ridiculous Chance's heart was known to be. He didn't know how to explain how badly he hated Jaxon playing witness to this fucked up mess. Garrett floated in and out of Chance's life like a one-man tornado, destroying everything in his path. It had been so long since he'd come around,

Chance had begun to hope for a normal life. A life with Jaxon. He should've known better.

Just one fucking time, Chance wanted to meet a man on equal footing—not be seen as weak or crazy. Then along came Garrett, ruining the only thing that mattered to Chance. His relationship with Jaxon. Since Jaxon was still staring at him, expecting an explanation, he knew he had to say something before Jaxon decided he wasn't worth his time. Chance would not do well in jail. In spite of Chance's less than stellar upbringing, he'd always believed he was above such things.

"I guess I hoped he'd go away on his

own without things escalating."

Jaxon shot him a disbelieving look. "Really, Chance? I didn't get but a minute with the guy, but it was obvious he's crazy as hell. And mean," Jaxon added after a moment. Another second passed before Jaxon added, "And stupid. All those things don't mix well."

Working up a bit of courage, Chance asked the one question weighing on his mind the heaviest, hoping to distract Jaxon. "Are you really going to arrest me?" After all, Jaxon hadn't read him his rights. Even though he'd never personally been taken into custody, Chance knew that was a requirement.

Jaxon blew out a sigh. "Since the

other dude is the one bleeding, normally, I wouldn't have a choice. Thankfully, the wood on your front door is splintered, so I can prove forced entry and you can claim self-defense."

Chance huffed, incredulous. "It *was* self-defense."

"I know that," Jaxon snapped.

Now that he wasn't worried about going to jail, Chance's smart mouth returned. "You sure have a funny way of showing it. I'm in the back of a police car, although you did spare me the handcuffs... pity."

Jaxon narrowed his eyes at him. Chance locked his back teeth to keep from saying another word. Lowering his chin, he stared at his lap, hoping to appear somewhat contrite. None of this was Jaxon's fault. He needed to remember that detail. One day, almost twelve months ago, Jaxon had stopped to help him change a flat tire on his car. Afterward, the man had followed Chance home, ensuring he made it safely. He'd been showing up every night since. It was hardly Jaxon's fault Chance had been a screwed up mess long before he came around — like starting at birth. The last thing he wanted was for Jaxon to give up on him.

Jaxon sighed, and when he spoke

again, his tone softened. "What happened today anyhow?"

Chance bit back a groan. He didn't want to lie, and if Jaxon kept this up, Chance wouldn't have a choice. An ache bloomed in the center of his chest. This man, he'd given Chance hope. For the first time in so long, he'd believed in something good. Getting involved with this would destroy everything about Jaxon that Chance loved. He couldn't do it. He shot a nervous glance at the camera mounted next to the rear view mirror. "Is that thing taping us?"

"It's always recording."

"Then I have nothing more to say." At his words, Jaxon turned his back on

Chance and pretended to bang his head on the steering wheel. Chance quickly looked away, hiding his smile. If his lowlife parents had taught him anything, it was to never let anyone get a confession on camera. Driving Jaxon insane was only a side benefit. The man needed someone to keep him on his toes. Damn, Jaxon looked sexy as hell in uniform. It was killing Chance. He wanted to run his fingers through Jaxon's dark hair, feel his hard body against his. Chance bit his lip to keep the moan in his head from slipping past his lips. It seemed wrong to want someone as much as Chance wanted Jaxon. The craving in his gut never lessened.

"Goddamn. Your landlord will have an aneurism when he sees your front door."

Jaxon's reminder of the mess they'd left behind pulled Chance's thoughts out of the gutter. He'd already thought of his landlord's reaction, and no way in hell was it happening. Considering the fact Chance was almost always late with his rent, he was already living by the man's good graces. Even if he had to do the repairs himself, Chance would have that door replaced before the landlord knew a thing.

"He'll never see it," Chance said as much for himself as Jaxon.

Jaxon sighed, sounding tired. "Whoever this guy is, maybe you should file a restraining order. You always attract the crazy ones. Too fucking sexy for your own goddamn good," Jaxon grumbled under his breath.

"It's nothing I can't handle."

"Chance," Jaxon began, and Chance cut him off, incapable of listening to anything Jaxon was about to say while using such a lecturing tone.

"Seriously, Jaxon. It's nothing I can't handle."

This was his problem. Not Jaxon's.

"It didn't look like you were handling it. After you smashed that lamp over his head, dude was enraged. What if I'd shown up five minutes later? Anything could've happened to you."

"Seeing you rushing in to save me didn't help matters," Chance said under his breath without thinking. He recognized his mistake the moment Jaxon's expression shifted, becoming calculating. Chance locked his teeth together to keep from saying anything else. Jaxon opened his mouth, and Chance snapped.

"I'm telling you, Garrett is harmless. For the most part."

He knew immediately he'd made a mistake. Jaxon expression turned thunderous. "Wait. You know this fucker?"

Chance shot another nervous glance at the dashboard cam. "Oh. For fuck's sake!" Jaxon growled, shouldering open his door with enough force, Chance felt sure he'd have a bruise later. After slamming it closed, Jaxon ripped his open and towed Chance from inside the car. He could tell Jaxon was taking great pains not to hurt him, but Jaxon was pissed. No doubt about it. Keeping one hand locked on his arm, Jaxon slammed the back door closed as well, making Chance wonder if it would ever reopen after such harsh treatment.

Chance eyed Jaxon warily. A flush covered Jaxon's cheeks and his eyes flashed with anger. The dark, slashing eyebrows, which normally made him look a little dangerous, made him seem downright deadly at the moment. In the year he'd known him, Chance had never truly seen Jaxon angry. He was now. It was hot. Goddamn. Chance knew it was ridiculous. No doubt it was also the worst timing ever, but the lust strumming through his veins couldn't be denied.

"All right. We're out of the car. No one can hear us. Now, tell me what the fuck is going on. Why are you refusing to take care of this? Take a fucking restraining order out, Chance."

Chance licked his lips, swearing he

could taste Jaxon's mouth lingering there. Damn, he needed to get the man alone. Jaxon's gaze dropped to Chance's mouth, following the motion. Without looking away, Jaxon took a step forward, forcing Chance to take one back. The car stopped him from going any farther. Jaxon's palms landed on either side of Chance as he boxed him in and crowded his space. In a show of nerves, Chance's chatterbox side made an appearance.

"I can't talk to you, Jaxon. Not inside your copzilla car, all tricked out with its sneaky cameras and not out here on the street where they're probably recording us from that car parked behind us." He thought it over before adding, "And that streetlight camera right there." He nodded toward it, just in case Jaxon didn't know what he meant. Jaxon didn't look. He was too busy towering over Chance wearing an unfathomable expression.

When Jaxon spoke, his voice rumbled from deep inside his chest. "I suggest you figure out where you can talk to me, because you are, one way or another." Casting a nervous look around, Chance spotted a mom-and-pop-type tuxedo rental place.

"Fine. In there," he said, grabbing Jaxon's hand and towing him toward the shop. He came willingly if not quietly.

"Oh, so, this place doesn't have any surveillance whatsoever?"

Since Jaxon couldn't see his face, Chance gave in to the smile growing inside him as he pushed through the door. Jaxon's smartass tone cracked him up. Tossing a glance over his shoulder, Chance answered his question. "Not inside the dressing rooms, they don't."

The older gentleman, who'd stood to greet them, took one look at Chance and switched his attention to Jaxon. Whatever the man saw in Jaxon's expression, he sat back down, taking up his spot on the barstool behind the counter. With a solid flick, he reopened his newspaper, shutting them out. Chance headed for the back of the store, finding the dressing room farthest away. He shoved Jaxon inside. It was a bit crowded when Chance joined him. Nonetheless, he pulled the door closed behind them, shutting out the world. Jaxon's face was smooth of all emotion, except for his eyes. Those were storm clouds, brewing with fire.

"Are you satisfied?"

Chance ignored Jaxon's sarcastic tone. "Not entirely. Take off your shirt."

Jaxon blinked. "Are you joking?"

"Not at all. For all I know, you're

wearing a wire. I want you out of that shirt." Chance bit the inside of his cheek to keep from bursting into laughter. Jaxon released a loud curse, but slid the buttons loose on his uniform. With it hanging open, exposing the white t-shirt beneath, he spread his arms wide.

"There. Are you happy?"

"No." Without giving Jaxon time to guess at his intentions, Chance shoved his hands beneath Jaxon's shirt and pushed it off the man's shoulders. Next came the t-shirt. Jaxon didn't protest as Chance tugged it over his head. With Jaxon's upper body bare, Chance ran his hands over Jaxon's every hardened line, even going as far as encircling the other man's waist and feeling up his back. Damn. Working out every day had done some delicious things to Jaxon's body.

Chance knew Jaxon wasn't wearing a wire. For fuck's sake. Did people even do such a thing nowadays? He had no idea. All Chance knew was he needed to feel Jaxon's skin against his. The adrenaline left behind from his run-in with Garrett was still rushing through Chance's veins. It combined with Chance's constant need to own this man who would never be his, leaving him half-crazed with lust.

Instead of attempting to explain himself to Jaxon, Chance conjured the memory of Jaxon's taste. He was like salty chocolate. He'd only tasted the other man's cock once before, months ago, but it had been enough to let Chance know one time would never be enough. His gaze locked on the deep valley in Jaxon's chest. Water filled his mouth.

"Maybe you'd like my pants too." The husky note in Jaxon's voice made Chance wonder if Jaxon was remembering that night as well. "After all, what's stopping me from having some way to record…"

Chance opened his mouth over the spot holding him captivated, cutting off Jaxon's speech. When Jaxon's arms encircled his waist, the power in the room shifted. Jaxon invaded his space, using his size against Chance. The erection pressing against his let Chance know Jaxon wasn't unaffected.

"Chance, I…"

He kissed him, shoving his tongue in Jaxon's mouth, licking away whatever argument he was about to make. Images filled Chance's head. He remembered every detail of the night they'd spent together. Jaxon's hands. The sounds Jaxon made as Chance took his dick down the back of his throat. The way Chance's heart had begged for more ever since. It was all right there. Cool air touched his back, making Chance realize Jaxon was pushing his shirt up. When Jaxon's fingers found his nipple, Chance's knees nearly gave out. A moan rose in his throat. Jaxon's lips moved to his jaw.

"Wearing a wire," Jaxon said with a laugh against his skin between kisses. Chance's fingers dug into Jaxon's back. He couldn't get close enough to the other man to appease his heart.

Tilting his head, giving Jaxon freer access to this throat, Chance soaked up the sensation of Jaxon's mouth against his neck. Chance's voice came out sounding breathless when he responded. "It worked, didn't it?" Jaxon shoved his hands down the back of his jeans, hauling Chance against him and making him realize how busy Jaxon's hands had been. He hadn't even felt Jaxon unbuttoning his jeans. Jaxon nipped at his shoulder.

"Your ploy only worked because I wanted it to. You should've been questioning a body camera."

Chance ground his erection against Jaxon's, losing himself with every scrape of material against his throbbing dick. "Are you wearing a body camera? That's kind of hot."

A soft knock landed on the door. Chance jumped away. Regret chilled his skin. Fuck. When would he grow up? He would end up costing Jaxon his job one of these days with his bullshit.

"As much as I hate to interrupt, I thought you might like to know that some long-haired punk, wearing all leather, just slashed the tires on your police cruiser."

At the shopkeeper's announcement, Chance threw open the door with such force it collided with Jaxon before he had time to get out of its way. A grunt of pain reverberated off the walls of the tiny room. The salesman's shocked expression almost gave Chance pause, making him wonder what the older man saw in his face. If it came anywhere near matching the rage in Chance's heart, then the man most likely feared for his life. He knew exactly who fit that description. Garrett was going down. It was one thing to fuck with him, but messing with Jaxon was going too far. He stormed from the room, buttoning his pants as he went. The man who'd delivered the news couldn't get out of Chance's way fast enough. His pulse beat in his ears and Chance's teeth locked, making it impossible for him to apologize. Following in his wake, Jaxon shoved his arms inside his shirt as they cleared the shop's door. To give himself something to do other than stare at Jaxon's gorgeous chest, Chance squatted down next to Jaxon's car, pretending to inspect the damage. Jaxon paced at Chance's back. The fury rolling off Jaxon's body hurt his heart, and he hated himself a little in that moment. Sometimes, Chance secretly wondered if he was cursed. All he did was destroy good people.

Jaxon growled. Seriously, growled. It came from the back of his throat, rumbling through the air. It was sexy as sin until he opened his mouth and ruined it.

"You know, for the life of me, I can't figure out why you always attract such fucking losers." Chance's heart skipped a beat. The air thickened, making it hard to breathe. "Seriously, Chance, this guy is obviously the lowest piece of shit." If only Jaxon had stopped there or if he'd been anyone else. Perhaps the words wouldn't have stabbed Chance through the heart. He was wrong. Jaxon had no clue what was really going on, but it didn't matter to the stupid organ in Chance's chest. The number of people whose opinion mattered to him was miniscule. Jaxon's cut to the bone. "Sometimes, you make such bullshit decisions, Chance. For a full fucking year, I've been trying to lock you down, but nope. You keep hitting the clubs and attracting every fucking crazy-ass, no-good bastard in a ten-mile radius. All this bullshit could've ended a long time ago if you'd just let me in, but you refuse. It's almost like you enjoy the attention." The realization that Jaxon thought badly of him, it was too much. Moving slowly, Chance pushed to his feet. To keep from balling his hands into fists, Chance brushed them down the front of his shirt, smoothing out the invisible wrinkles. He tried hard to rearrange his features, hoping against hope Jaxon wouldn't see his anger.

Unfortunately, his efforts did nothing to cover the rage in his voice when Chance finally found it. "You're right, of course. I'm a huge idiot. First off for thinking I'm a grown-ass man who shouldn't need a piece of paper from the courts to convince another grown-ass man to stay away from me. But mostly, I'm a huge dumbass for believing someone like you could ever lower yourself enough to be with an attention whore like me."

Jaxon ran both hands through his hair, making Chance wonder if he considered pulling it out. "What the hell is wrong with you?"

"I thought we established that already," Chance said, sounding ridiculously calm, even to his ears. "I'm an idiot, remember?"

Jaxon ignored his question. "Aren't you the same person who was in that dressing room with me? It seems I wanted to be with you pretty damn badly not even five minutes ago."

Chance was shaking his head before Jaxon finished his claim. "You want my body, but you don't want me. Not that I blame you," he added in case Jaxon thought he was waiting for him to deny it. Truly, Chance understood. "If I had a choice, it wouldn't be me either. You have a good job and life. I have nothing to show for anything except some crazy fucker who won't leave me alone, a broken front door I can't afford to get fixed, and too much affection for a cop who thinks I'm too stupid to take care of myself. So you're right, I'm a bad bet." Jaxon's hands rose before falling back to his sides, as if proving he had nothing. It was for the best. "Do me a favor, please? Stay away from me. My heart can't stand caring about someone who thinks so little of me."

Without waiting for Jaxon to give his word, Chance turned away, already calculating the cost of repairing his door. He needed to focus on reality. Dreaming only made his life seem that much bleaker. Best he concentrate on putting one foot in front of the other. It was a long walk to the library where he worked, and Chance was already ten minutes late.

*

Chance always made him crazy, and Jaxon was hooked. It had been almost a year since he'd pulled in behind Chance's car on the side of the road. Their gazes had met, and he hadn't looked away since. The man's green eyes, auburn hair, and runner's body aside, Chance was beautiful on the inside. Of course, it was hidden beneath a layer of insanity covered with a coating of conspiracy theorist, but it was there for anyone who bothered to look.

It had taken Jaxon almost eight months to corner Chance into a kiss, and another two to coax him into bed. He hadn't been back since. Jaxon kept showing up. Chance kept letting him in, but that was where things ended. No matter how hard he tried, or how turned on they both were after a night of doing everything except the deed, Chance shut him down at every turn — until today. Jaxon didn't doubt for a minute he'd have been fucking Chance inside that dressing room if they hadn't been interrupted. Of course, he'd fucked that up quick. It had been as simple as opening his mouth. Jaxon's temper had always been his biggest downfall.

As much as Jaxon was tempted to chase Chance down the street, making a total ass of himself, he still had a job to do. Not to mention, he knew from experience Chance was best left alone when he was angry. That didn't mean Jaxon was giving up. Whether Chance wanted to admit it or not, he belonged to Jaxon. It was time for Chance to accept it. He was tired of playing games. Every time he heard Chance laugh, saw him smile – hell, just caught the man's eye – Jaxon had to stop himself from confessing every growing feeling inside his head. Almost a year. Jaxon wasn't stupid — didn't try deluding himself. He was in love with Chance. No one else would do.

With a growl, Jaxon pulled his phone from his belt and called in reinforcements. Three rings sounded in his ear before Sam answered.

"Yep."

Jaxon spent a moment restraining himself from lecturing Sam on how to answer a phone. Considering his natural condescension for others had already alienated one person today, he skipped it. "I need a favor."

"Yep."

Biting back a snort, Jaxon reminded himself that Sam was one huge fucker who could squash him with the bare minimum of effort. "If you roll down Highway 30, you'll find Chance looking murderous. He should've been at work a good fifteen minutes ago. Can you pick him up and make it look like you happened upon him? If he knows I sent you, he'll keep walking just to spite me."

"Showed your ass again, huh?"

"Like the expert I am."

The silence blaring through the line almost had Jaxon wishing he hadn't called. Almost. Chance having a way to work was more important than Jaxon's pride. Finally, Sam sighed. The sound said a thousand things that Sam, thankfully, kept to himself.

"Anything I need to know about?"

For a moment, Jaxon considered telling the man to mind his business, but Chance was his concern. "Some dude tried busting through his front door this morning. Chance broke a lamp over his head."

"Let me guess," Sam said, cutting

him off. "You told him how stupid he was for not filing charges or some shit."

"Not in so many words."

Sam blew out a sigh. "Jesus. Okay. I'm headed his way."

Jaxon's shoulders relaxed. "Thanks, man. I owe you one."

"You don't owe me shit, but it sounds like you owe Chance an apology. I realize you don't know as much as you should about Chance, and that's not on you, but Chance is solid as hell. He puts up with a lot of shit from a lot of people for reasons that are entirely his own. I like you, dude. I really do, but you don't respect Chance, and that's the truth."

Possibly if Sam didn't have ninety pounds of solid muscle on Jaxon, Jaxon might've challenged his claim. Unfortunately, he knew Sam cared about Chance. That superseded any amount of bruised pride on Jaxon's part.

Biting back all the things he wanted to say, Jaxon chose a different argument instead. "He shuts me out, and that's the truth."

Sam snorted. "He shuts everyone out. That's his thing. Chance doesn't need you to fix him, because he's not broken. He needs you to love him, because that's what he's missing."

"I do."

"Show it," Sam said before the line went silent, letting Jaxon know the man said goodbye the same way he said hello.

Chapter 2

When the car pulled in alongside him, Chance turned, ready to blast Jaxon, only to find a different familiar face staring out at him from behind the steering wheel. Samuel Wilson had known Chance longer than anyone, since back before the string of bad decisions that lead him here. The man was roughly the size of a small dump truck, but he was a gentle giant. It was easy to see the kindness in his sweet brown eyes.

"I thought I recognized that sexy ass." Sam didn't mean it. Even still, Chance couldn't deny the compliment was a cooling balm on his bruised pride. "Can I give you a lift somewhere?"

Chance ran his hands through his hair. Blowing out a sigh, he gave in. "Yeah, thanks. Normally, I wouldn't put you out, but I'm already super late to work," Chance said, climbing into the passenger seat of the F150. "I really appreciate this. It's been one hell of a day already."

"No worries, man," Sam said, pulling away from the curb. "As it happens, I was on my way to see you at the library when I spotted you walking down the street." Sam cast a sly look his way. "Want to tell me what's up?"

"Not really, no."

"Does it have anything to do with all the police cars sitting at your house or your busted front door?" Before Chance had time to inquire, Sam answered his unspoken question. "Yeah, I swung by there first, hoping to catch you before work. Obviously, you weren't there, but I saw the mess."

Chance barely suppressed the urge to bang his head on the window. "Fuck. I need to get that door fixed before someone calls the landlord or steals all my stuff, but goddamn. I can't afford this shit, especially if I lose my fucking job." Chance scrubbed his hand across his forehead, hoping to wipe away the pain blooming there.

"Garrett again?"

"Yep," Chance said, sounding dead even to his ears.

Sam changed lanes before heading in the opposite direction. "Where're we going?"

"To get you a new door. Call the library and let them know you'll be late."

Chance stared at Sam's profile in disbelief. "Um, thanks, but even if I had my wallet with me, or my phone, for that matter, which I don't since Jaxon shoved me into the back of his patrol car this morning before I could grab anything, I can't really afford a new door today. I'll figure something out."

After a second of digging around in his console, Sam came out with a phone. He passed it Chance's way. "Call the library. I've got you covered on the door. This weekend, there's a competition up Washington way. That's why I was headed to see you. If you're game, I'd love for you to go with me and work as my assistant. Your pay would cover the door and then some."

Sam was amazing. One day, he would make some dude really happy. If anyone snagged him.

"You know I'm in. Whatever you need."

Without looking away from the road, Sam dipped his chin. "Just let work know you'll be there as soon as we're done, and thanks for helping me out this weekend. Sometimes, not having anyone in my corner is a bigger handicap than anything else."

Personally, Chance thought Sam was feeding him a load of shit, covering up how much he was helping Chance, but whatever. Chance couldn't turn down the work. Plus, the Strong Man circuit was a blast to follow, and Sam was a damn good competitor. In Chance's opinion, it was only a matter of time before Sam took over the world.

In an unusual burst of nosiness, Sam broached the taboo. "So Jaxon shoved you in the back of patrol car, huh? How did that go?" Chance shot an annoyed look Sam's way, but held his tongue. Sam chuckled. "That well, huh? You ever going to tell the man the truth about Garrett?"

"Not if I can help it."

"Do you mind if I ask why?"

Chance's first reaction was hell yeah, he minded, but Sam already knew all his bullshit and was currently doing him a huge favor. It seemed too much like a dickhead move to tell the man to mind his own fucking business.

"Jaxon is a good man with a stellar reputation. I don't want to sully that. If he knew anything about me, he'd try to fix me, and just no."

Sam held on to his opinion until the count of five, which was longer than Chance expected. "See, the problem with all that is he wants to be with you. I don't see him giving up on that, especially since you want him too." Sam glanced over and winked. "No man in his right mind would walk away from such a hot piece of ass."

Chance shook his head. "Sometimes, I wonder what you do with your time when you're not pretending to want me."

"I'm stroking my sister-in-law's ego," Sam said, surprising Chance with his answer. "You know I can't let other men get too lax with their hotties. It's not fair to us single folk."

Before that moment, Chance had always assumed Sam was only into men. Never in his life had Chance wanted to ask a question as badly as he wanted to inquire over this tidbit. He bit his lip and stared straight ahead, trying to hold it in.

A low chuckle rumbled through the truck, sounding wicked as hell. "Yeah. I go both ways," Sam said, sparing Chance from his curiosity.

Shrugging, Chance did his best to pretend as if the question never crossed his mind. "Whatever, man. You know I don't give a shit." Sam's knowing laughter chaffed, but Chance would survive it.

Sam waited patiently while Chance called the library. Luck was on his side. It turned out they were having an extra slow day and had intended to send him home as soon as he arrived. Problem solved. At least something had gone his way. As Chance handed the phone back to Sam, the device buzzed in his hand. Sam glanced at the screen before tucking it away.

"You care if I make a quick stop before we hit the home store?"

Chance shrugged. "I've got nothing else going on."

"Cool," Sam said, changing directions once more. After ten minutes of silence, Sam pulled into the gym. "Let's go. I need to pay my dues. You're not sitting here sulking while I'm gone."

Shouldering open the door, Chance rolled his eyes. The brick and glass building appeared like any other structure on Spring Avenue. Most people drove past Smith Brothers' Fight Club every day without realizing some of the world's greatest competitors trained inside. Everyone, from professional body builders to MMA champions to Strong Man competitors like Sam, breezed through the door on a daily basis.

It was where Chance met Sam several years earlier after Adam's abandonment. If not for Sam, Chance didn't like to think about where he would've ended up. But that was Sam. He was a lost-cause collector. Sam took in broken souls like most people did baseball cards. Secretly, Chance thought it was Sam's penchant for honesty that drew people to him. When someone had been beaten down and lied to their entire life, it was refreshing as hell to have someone around who always spoke the truth, even when it hurt. Sam bypassed the front desk.

"What happened to paying your dues?"

"I'll get to it," Sam said without bothering to glance Chance's way.

Biting back a sigh, Chance followed on Sam's heels. When Chance caught sight of Sam's destination, Holden Fontaine, he swallowed down a groan and nearly changed directions. At five-foot-nine, Chance was accustomed to men towering over him. As a matter of point, he looked ridiculous standing next to Sam, who at six feet and six inches, stared at the tops of everyone's heads. Holden was one of the few men who could meet Chance's eye. That is, if the man ever met anyone's gaze. He was beautiful like a porcelain doll, but skittish. Those two things combined to make Chance uncomfortable as fuck every second he spent in the man's company. When Holden caught a glimpse of them moving in his direction, his gaze skirted in every direction, as if seeking an escape. Sam didn't take mercy on him.

"I got your text."

In a show of bravery Chance had never witnessed before, Holden visibly squared his shoulders, and met Sam's stare. "You shouldn't be surprised. I already told you I probably wouldn't go this weekend."

Fuck. Chance didn't want to be here, witnessing whatever was going on between the two.

Sam shrugged. "I'm not worried over it. Chance has already agreed to go with me," Sam said, motioning Chance's way and dragging him into things. "My issue is how you couldn't tell me to my face, so here I am."

In spite of his discomfort, Chance's gaze continued to move between the pair, and he soaked up every word. He'd never heard Sam speak a word in anger to anyone. Normally, the man's size deterred any arguments. Holden focused on him, making Chance grateful for all the times the other man hadn't met his gaze before now. The man's sea green stare was intense and uncomfortable. It took every ounce of strength he possessed not to look away.

"Thank you for going with Sam this weekend. It really sucks when he has to go alone. Not that he ever has," Holden said bitterly, switching his attention back to Sam.

"Um, sure thing," Chance said, but Holden and Sam had already forgotten his existence. Even Chance had lost interest in his part of the conversation. The way Holden's jaw ticked fascinated him. This man who always seemed scared of his own shadow was facing off against one of the world's strongest men, and damned if he didn't look ready to fight without an ounce of fear.

"Did you get what you were after?

I'm in your face, saying I won't go, and you got to rub another man in my face. You can go now."

Chance opened his mouth to argue he wasn't any kind of "other man" when it came to Sam, but Sam's malicious smile caused the words to die on his lips.

"Yeah. I got exactly what I came for—you showing for half a second that I matter at all."

Before Holden had time to react, Sam snagged Chance's arm and steered him toward the door. As they passed the front desk again, Chance fought the urge to point out Sam still hadn't paid his dues. He didn't believe for a second that was why they were there.

Sam sat behind the wheel for five minutes, staring into space before acknowledging Chance's presence again. When he finally glanced Chance's way, a blatantly false smile stretched Sam's lips.

"You know what we need?"

Chance had to know. "What?"

Sam started the truck. "A break from dumbass men who don't know our worth. Want to hit C.J.'s after we fix your door?"

Since alcohol did indeed feel like the answer to all his problems at the moment, Chance didn't hesitate. "Hell yeah."

Chapter 3

Three hours of radio silence from Sam had Jaxon ready to crawl out of his skin. At the very least, he wanted to ditch his shift and chase Chance down. No one understood how Chance was everything. Putting his foot in his mouth and fucking things up was Jaxon's usual method of dealing with life, but when it came to Chance, Jaxon hated himself more in these moments than ever before. In his defense, it had been months since he'd had any ass. It was Chance or no one, and Chance kept shutting him down. When his phone rang, flashing Sam's number at him, Jaxon had to stop himself from crushing the phone in his impatience.

"Did you find him?"

"Damn. Is that how you answer a phone?"

Jaxon thought he might've blacked out for a minute at Sam's lecture. He also feared the eye-twitching he was currently experiencing might become a permanent disability. Still, he recognized Sam had done him a favor.

"Hello, Sam. Did you find him?"

Sam chuckled. Bastard. He knew exactly what he was about. "Of course. He's good. We got his door all fixed up, and I'm heading back over to pick him up in two hours. I imagine if you head C.J.'s way in a few hours, you'll trip over us there."

Jaxon swallowed down the relief raging through him, hoping his desperation didn't show in his tone. "Thanks, man. I appreciate it more than words."

"Yep," Sam said, disconnecting their call before Jaxon could continue. Jaxon was too relieved to fucking care about Sam's phone etiquette.

Four hours later, Jaxon found himself sitting inside C.J.'s dance hall, staring Chance down like a crazed stalker. The only thing saving an ounce of his pride was the fact that every other male eye in the building was also upon him. Unfortunately, he could also see the vultures closing in. If he didn't pick up the pace, someone else would take Jaxon's place. Unfortunately, he wasn't sure about his welcome. After all, Chance had asked him to stay away from him. Problem was, Jaxon couldn't do that. It was the one thing Jaxon would never be able to give Chance.

As he pushed his way through the crowd, intent on reaching Chance, Jaxon wondered how the other man couldn't feel his stare boring into the back of his head. Even to him, it was over-the-top intense. The way Chance's jeans cupped his delicious ass to perfection was partially to blame for the hunger gnawing at Jaxon's gut. The rest of the fault lay with his heart. It belonged to Chance.

"Can I buy you a drink?"

Chance jumped at least six inches in his surprise when Jaxon spoke against his ear. A smile—one that seemed to come from the man's soul—crossed Chance's face until he obviously remembered he was pissed off at Jaxon. "You could, but I wouldn't accept."

"What if I convinced them to put extra whipped cream on top?" He knew the way to Chance's heart. He had a bad sweet tooth. Personally, Jaxon only enjoyed whipped cream one way and food had nothing to do with it. Jaxon could tell by Chance's expression he was about to get shut down. Chance's hips were sliding across Jaxon's palms before even he knew he'd reached for the sexy man. "You don't want anything from me. I get that. Would you do something else for me, then?"

*

Chance would do anything for Jaxon. God help him because no one else would. Why did Jaxon have to be so damn sexy? Chance wanted to cling to his anger. It was easier than his hurt.

"Dance with me?"

Chance eyed the way Jaxon's t-shirt

strained against his muscles. Weak. He was weak. By the time Chance realized he'd silently accepted, he was already in the center of the dance floor. Jaxon pulled him closer and spun, making Chance laugh. "Quit mooning at me. You'll make people suspicious. Remember. For all most people know, we met here for the first time tonight." Chance rolled his eyes at Jaxon's ridiculousness. This was the side of him Chance couldn't resist... as if there was any side of Jaxon he could stand against. "Ah. Much better," Jaxon said, making Chance's stomach muscles clench in anticipation as Jaxon's deep voice vibrated against his skin. "Now it looks like I've said something outrageous, but not too much so since you didn't knee me in the balls and storm away. You're intrigued. Interested." In spite of himself, Chance laughed. "Perfect," Jaxon said, flashing Chance a wicked smile. "I'm making a good impression. No one will bat an eye when you leave with me tonight. I'm an obvious catch."

"Jaxon," Chance breathed.

Jaxon's eyebrow lifted in question, just the one, exactly as he'd always done. A wave of longing crashed over Chance, making it impossible for him to continue. God only knew how much he craved the man in his arms. Jaxon's face softened. The smile never faltered. "I just want to be close to you," he said, leaving Chance stunned. "But you keep me at arm's length. That's why I was so aggravated today. Ever since the night we spent together, you shut me down at every turn. I think about you all the time." His gaze shifted to Chance's mouth. "I want to kiss you." The power of his hunger nearly caused Chance's stomach to growl at Jaxon's confession. He didn't stop there. "In my mind, your sweet tongue brushes against mine. Every time I've tasted you still lives in my head. I can remember every detail, the sounds you make when I touch you."

"All my bad decisions," Chance said, cutting in and reminding Jaxon of why they'd argued.

Jaxon didn't back down. "Give me your bullshit, Chance. There isn't anything you could've possibly done in your lifetime that would make me think badly of you." It was physically painful how desperately he wanted to believe. Chance kept his gaze locked on Jaxon's chest to stop the other man from seeing the longing in his eyes. "Chance, look at me." Incapable of denying him, he did as Jaxon bade. His pained expression begged for Chance's understanding. "When I got the call to your address this morning, my heart stopped. I couldn't get to you fast enough. Then I get there, and there's blood everywhere." He shook his head as if there were no words. "You got a firsthand look at the temper that has kept every other man before you away."

That was the biggest line of bullshit Chance had ever heard. "You're the nicest person I know."

"See? That right there says more about your life than any of the stories you've told me. I'm not nice at all. Hell. Half the time, I can't even stand the sound of other people's voices. I'm cranky as hell and secretly think everyone's an idiot. You're the only exception. When it comes to you, I can't get enough of listening to you. You're the most intelligent and strongest person

I've ever met. I'm going to say things I don't mean, and I'm going to fuck up. Trust me. I know you deserve a better man than me, but no one else will ever love you more than I do."

The song ended and a second slow song slid in behind it. Jaxon pulled Chance closer, filling the final gap between them. Chance stared at Jaxon in disbelief. "Did you really just drop the 'L' word on me?"

Jaxon didn't look the least bit scared or ashamed. "Hell yeah."

"Careful," Chance whispered when he found his voice again. "People will see your heart in your eyes and wonder if we met before tonight." Jaxon's low laugh rumbled in his chest, bringing a smile to Chance's lips.

"Oh, baby, nobody is watching us. They're all looking at their phones."

As if the universe decided to make a liar of him, someone shoved Jaxon from behind with enough force that it almost knocked both of them over.

"Look who it is."

The sound of Garrett's voice caused a chill to race over Chance. Jaxon spun. Chance had both hands wrapped around his shirt, intent on holding the man back in an instant. Jaxon glanced over his shoulder with one eyebrow raised and a smirk hovering on his lips.

"Really?"

Chance shrugged. "You said you had a temper." Even when Jaxon switched his attention back to Garrett, Chance didn't let go.

"What can I help you with?" Jaxon sounded so damn calm.

Garrett snorted. With his blond hair pulled back away from his face and muscles flexing on the crowd's behalf, Garrett was getting more than his fair share of looks from the other men in the club. If only they knew how ugly Garrett was on the inside, Chance thought bitterly. "You can get the fuck out of my way. This has nothing to do with you."

Chance and Jaxon snorted simultaneously.

Garrett ignored Chance, but took a step closer to Jaxon at the open challenge. Jaxon was off duty, but still, Chance wondered if Garrett was stupid enough to throw a punch at a cop.

"Then again, maybe you are the problem. Before my little brother took up with you, he understood his place in our family." Chance bit back a groan. He hadn't wanted Jaxon to find out this way. Unfortunately, Garrett was still talking, ringing the death knoll on his chances with Jaxon. "Now that's he's fucking Detective Do-Good, he thinks he too good to help out a brother in need."

Chance was still trying to work out Garrett's dumbass reasoning when Jaxon glanced over his shoulder again. Laughter shone heavily in his gaze. Chance couldn't decide if it was genuine or if he was covering up his surprise. "Guess I know what this morning was about now. You were trying to knock the stupid out of him."

There weren't enough lamps in the world.

Somehow, Garrett shifted an inch closer until he was almost bumping chests with Jaxon. "You think being a cop keeps you safe? Meet me outside without your badge and we'll see who the real man is here. Maybe once Chance sees how big of a pussy you really are, he'll stop thinking with his dick."

Jaxon tensed as if he meant to accept Garrett's challenge. Chance couldn't have that. Not only had he had enough of Garrett's bullying, there was no way he would let Jaxon risk his career over such a piece of shit. Digging his keys from his pocket, Chance reached past Jaxon and hit Garrett with six million volts from his key chain Taser. Garrett went down. Hard. Keeping his keys hidden, Chance went down on his knees beside him.

"Oh my God. I think he's having a

seizure." He caught a flash of surprise on Jaxon's features before he focused on Garrett's face, blocking out the man he loved for the one who'd used him and stolen from him for as long as Chance could remember. He lowered his voice for Garrett's ears alone. "If you ever come near me or mine again, you won't walk away next time, understood?" Chance hit him with the Taser again just to be sure Garrett knew he wasn't playing. Jaxon pulled Chance to his feet before he could hit Garrett a third time.

"Let's go," Jaxon said against his ear, dragging him toward the door. Chance kept his gaze locked on Garrett's stunned face until he couldn't see the man any longer. Chance needed his brother to understand he would see him dead if ever threatened Jaxon again.

*

Jaxon was more than a little surprised when Chance lasted ten minutes in the silence of his truck without breaking. Normally, he was a nervous chatterer.

"Are you mad?"

Jaxon shook his head. "I'm not mad."

"The muscle in your jaw says otherwise. It's ticking."

Most likely it was because Jaxon was

trying to hold back his laughter. Garrett's challenge meant nothing to him. Dozens of people got in his face on a daily basis. It came with the job. He'd never met anyone like Chance. He'd zapped the bastard in a heartbeat when he'd threatened Jaxon. No one ever tried coming to his rescue. Chance would be the death of him, but he was going down with a smile. This man was the sexiest case of insanity Jaxon had ever encountered. A smile tugged at his lips. He was incapable of stopping it. Any other man might run for the hills in the face of Chance's craziness. Jaxon couldn't get enough. Of course, that didn't mean they didn't have things to discuss.

"So Garrett's your brother."

Jaxon hadn't meant it as a question, but Chance treated it as one.

"Yeah."

"You Tased your brother for me."

Out of the corner of his eye, Jaxon saw Chance shift in his seat, obviously uncomfortable with the topic. "Yeah, well, he wouldn't hesitate to hurt me."

Jaxon drove another mile in silence, attempting to call his rage under control before saying anything else. The idea that Chance's brother would harm him warred with Jaxon's fury over Chance having such a shitty family. He'd never met anyone who deserved the world like Chance did, yet from birth, people shit all over him. It was no wonder Chance didn't believe he could trust Jaxon to take care of him. No one put Chance first. That stopped now. "I'm not sure why you didn't think you could tell me that." He left it at that, because he didn't want to fight. Since Chance had gone all this time without explaining Garrett, Jaxon wasn't expecting Chance to start now. He was more than a little surprised when Chance responded.

"I knew from the moment we met, losing you would devastate me. So I kept you at arm's length. I thought if I could keep you as a friend, my heart wouldn't break when you realized how fucked up my life really is. Then you kissed me, and I was hooked. I was also terrified."

"Why?"

Jaxon glanced over in time to see Chance shrug, but the man didn't meet his gaze.

"You're amazing, and you have this great job that's the perfect fit for you. Seriously, it's like you were born to help people. All I have is shit I'm barely hanging on to and a fucked up family. They show up periodically, stealing everything they can, hoping to buy as much drugs as they can before landing back in jail. I don't want that for you.

You deserve better. At least, that's what I tell myself, but I still can't stay away. The night we made love. Fuck. It was." Chance didn't finish. He didn't need to. Jaxon knew. It had been earth shattering. Jaxon couldn't lose Chance over something neither of them could control.

"Everyone has pieces of shit hanging in their family tree. I have a younger sister in prison for hitting and killing a teenager while driving drunk. There's an uncle on my dad's side who everyone knows cooks meth and beats his kids. I can't control those things and I don't for one second think they reflect on me."

"But those people aren't banging

down your door every other day. If you're with me, my brother will be in your face and life forever. What if he costs you your job? I love you too much to hurt you like that."

Jaxon couldn't let this go on. He really couldn't, especially not on the heels of Chance saying he loved him. "I like my job, but it's just that. A job. I found it when I was looking for one, and if I lose it, which won't happen over this shit, then I'll find another one. You never know, I might find something I like better. But you found me when I wasn't looking, and if I lose you, there will never be anyone capable of replacing you. This past year with you." Jaxon shook his head, incapable of thinking of a word strong enough to describe how happy he'd been since meeting Chance. "I've lived long enough to know not everyone finds what I have in you. Every time we kiss, I'm undone."

"Pull over."

At Chance's panicked demand, Jaxon shot a nervous glance in his direction. Turned sideways in his seat, he was staring at Jaxon's profile.

"Are you okay?"

"I'm fine." Chance shook his head, belying his words. "Pull over." His voice shook on the final syllable, and Jaxon maneuvered to the side of the road. In all the time he'd known Chance, he'd never witnessed the man showing a moment's weakness. It scared the hell out of him. The second his truck was in park, Chance was out of his seatbelt and straddling Jaxon's hips. His tongue curled around Jaxon's, fighting for dominance. Jaxon's cock lengthened, beating against his zipper, and begging to be closer to Chance.

Ragged breaths filled the air. The warm globes of Chance's ass filled Jaxon's hands as he found his way inside the other man's jeans. His own jeans loosened, making Jaxon realize Chance was doing his best to strip Jaxon out of his clothing. Tearing his mouth away, Jaxon tried desperately to draw air into his starving lungs. The darkened street where they sat was almost dead this time of night, but still.

"They're probably recording this from that red-light camera over there."

Chance nipped at his neck, obviously unconcerned by Jaxon's claim. "Good. Everyone who works in that department will know you belong to me." When Chance's fingers encircled Jaxon's erection, Jaxon no longer cared who witnessed it. Electricity crackled and popped between them as their lips clashed—hard and hot. "Please tell me there's a condom somewhere in this truck."

"Glove box," Jaxon hissed out between clenched teeth.

Chance leaned over and dug through the glove box. "That's odd."

"Not really," he said, even though he wasn't in the mood to argue the complexities of his mind. He stayed so hard for Chance all the time, there was no way in hell he'd ever go anywhere unprepared. Chance's hands shook as he pried his jeans off and helped Jaxon suit up. Need clawed at his spine, making Jaxon insane. By the time the lower half of Chance was bare and he lowered himself onto Jaxon's needy cock, Jaxon was ready to tear at his skin. One glance at Chance's dilated eyes and parted lips caused Jaxon's impatience to bleed away. He was the reason for the flush on Chance's cheeks. When Chance rocked against him, Jaxon's mind went blank. He was nothing more than hunger and need in the arms of satiation and abundance. Chance was perfection.

Chance pressed his forehead to Jaxon's as they both gasped for air. The sound caressed Jaxon's ears like his favorite song. "I love you, Jaxon." The words on Chance's lips caused something inside him to snap. Snagging Chance's ass, he hauled the other man forward as he surged upward, making sure to hit at the right angle to drive Chance insane. They were too fucking big to be trying this shit in a truck on the side of the road. Not to mention how much shit Jaxon would be in if they got caught. None of those things meant a damn thing with Chance holding his stare, pumping his own cock, and dragging Jaxon closer to insanity. Chance's ass was so hot and tight. Jaxon's mind was stuck on repeat. All he could hear was the constant chant running round his brain. *Oh my God. I love this man. I love this man. Holy fuck. He loves me too.* Cupping the back of Chance's head, Jaxon held him in place, ensuring he couldn't look away. Even as the ecstasy of pressure drew his balls up tight, climbing up his cock, and threatening to fill the condom between them, Jaxon didn't look away. His mouth went dry. He could barely breath. Even his skin felt too tight. The edge of orgasm with Chance was a beautiful place to be.

"I've always loved you," Jaxon swore, never meaning anything more in his life.

A cry broke past Chance's lips as his orgasm hit. Hot cum coated Jaxon's shirt, soaking through to his skin. Jaxon didn't give a fuck. With Chance's soft hair held tightly between his fingers, and the man's eyes locked on his, Jaxon buried himself deep in Chance's ass. Every breath was hard won, even with Chance's scent filling his nose. As

Chance rode out the waves of his orgasm in Jaxon's arms, Jaxon knew nothing could tear them apart. This crazy, out-of-control life with Chance was exactly what he'd always dreamed of having. Being with Chance made him complete

Epilogue

With his shoulders braced against the wall, his foot resting on the lip of the tub, and a deluge of water slipping down the front of his body, Chance reveled in the way Jaxon fucked him. Keeping his eyes closed, Chance absorbed every sensation. The cold shower wall, competing with the hot water. Jaxon's thick cock stretched his asshole wide as he pounded away at the knot inside Chance and threatened to send him soaring into heaven. Jaxon's tongue felt like a lash of fire as it scraped along Chance's nipple. Chance's fingers flexed, indulging in their place against

Jaxon's shoulders. The way the other man's muscles tensed and rolled beneath Chance's palms added to the mountain of passion coursing through Chance's veins. When his orgasm hit, and his cock twitched with each jet of semen leaving it, tiny sparks of electricity popped behind Chance's closed lids like a firework show.

Jaxon moaned against Chance's chest as Chance's hungry ass convulsed around the man's cock, attempting to pull him deeper. The desperate sound sent another wave of pleasure crashing over Chance, threatening to take his knees out. Jaxon kept them upright, even as he joined Chance in the madness.

By the time they'd clean their mess away, and Chance's overheated body slid between the cool sheets, he was more than half asleep. When Jaxon slipped into bed beside him, Chance automatically rolled into the other man's waiting arms. The instant their bodies collided, Chance's mind came awake like he'd ingested three hits of speed. It raced and chased everything that happened that day.

He couldn't believe this man loved him. He'd been so scared for so long. Now, in retrospect, Chance realized he should've known Jaxon was too strong to let Garrett take them down. He should've known Jaxon would stand with him through anything.

A hint of guilt wormed its way into his mind. "I went with Sam to C.J.'s." Chance felt more than saw Jaxon's focus upon him, but he didn't respond. "I forgot to let him know I was leaving with you."

"Don't worry over Sam," Jaxon said, sounding more asleep than awake. "I imagine he was too busy chasing Holden to worry over you."

That was true. His relief lasted only long enough for Jaxon's words to truly sink in, and then his brain carried him back through the day once more.

"You plotting sons-of-bitches."

Jaxon's laughter vibrated against Chance's skin as his arms tightened around Chance's body. Chance smiled into the dark. Thank God, Sam was secretly a meddling bastard. Chance couldn't be happier with being managed.

The End.

If you enjoyed this book, please consider leaving a review.

Keep an eye out for book two, Uneven.

A Few More Books by Charity Parkerson:
Collide (M/M, Sports Romance)

Blow (M/M, Cop, Sports Romance)

Thrash (M/M, Sports Romance)

Shatter (M/M, Sports Romance)

Crush (M/M, Sports Romance)

Undone (M/M, Sports Romance, Cop)

Heart's Beat (M/M, Rockstar Romance)

Heart's Song (M/M, Rockstar Romance)

Heart's Strum (M/M, Rockstar Romance)

Heart's Duo (M/M, F/M, Rockstar Romance)

Heart's Chord (M/M, Military, Rockstar Romance)

Sated (M/F/M, F/M, M/M/M/F, Cop, Rockstar, Dark Romance)

Spent (M/F/M, M/M/F, F/M Dark Romance, Paranormal)

Inoperative (F/M, Sci-Fi Erotica)

Intact (F/M, M/M, Sci-Fi Erotic)

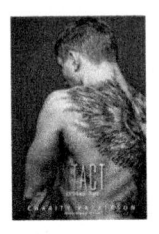

A Splash of Hope (F/M, Spicy Romantic Suspense)

A Dash of Desire (F/M, Spicy Romantic Suspense)